JEFFREY AND
THE THIRD-GRADE GHOST
Pet Day Surprise

Other Jeffrey and the Third-Grade Ghost Books

BOOK FOUR

Pet Day Surprise

Megan Stine
AND
H. William Stine

FAWCETT COLUMBINE
NEW YORK

To Joe Arthur—
for fat cats and funny dogs.
Arf! Meow! Get down, Shag—Nasty!

JEFFREY AND
THE THIRD-GRADE GHOST
Pet Day Surprise

Chapter One

"I don't care what you have in that box," Melissa McKane said to Benjamin Hyde as they walked to school. "It could never be as good as Jeffrey's report was."

"Yeah," said Kenny Thompsen. "Really cool, Jeffrey. A squirt-gun fight right in class. I couldn't believe it."

Jeffrey Becker smiled. He knew his best friends—Ben, Melissa, and Kenny—were all going to give terrific science reports in Mrs. Merrin's third-grade class. But none of them could be as cool as his report had been yesterday. Even Jeffrey had to admit it.

"It wasn't a squirt-gun fight," Jeffrey explained. "It was a scientific report on water pressure. I think it's a step forward for education. You get just as wet as in a squirt-gun fight, but you learn more."

"I died when you said that to Mrs. Merrin," Kenny said.

Melissa did a cartwheel on the sidewalk. "She

must really like you. What other teacher would let you squirt her?"

"I had to do it," Jeffrey said, grinning. "It was my proof that water pressure is strongest when the squirt gun is full."

A cold February wind blew, and Ben pulled his down jacket around the shoe box he was carrying.

"Do me a favor," Ben said to Jeffrey. "Don't become a researcher when you grow up. I don't think the world is ready for a scientist with your kind of mind."

Jeffrey laughed. He and Ben had been a team ever since kindergarten. Ben was going to be a scientist when he grew up. His wild inventions were great at getting the two of them into trouble. And Jeffrey's stories were great at getting them out of it.

"So what's in the box, Ben?" Jeffrey asked.

"A thamnophis," Ben answered, as if everyone knew what that was.

"In English, Ben," Jeffrey said.

"A thamnophis," Ben explained, "is another name for a garden snake. My report is on snakes, and I'm bringing in a prime specimen." Ben pushed his gold-rimmed glasses back on his nose.

4

"Can I hold him, please?" asked Melissa.

"Her," Ben said. "But I'm not opening the box. I don't want Miranda to get cold."

"Did you know that Arvin Pubbler is actually scared of snakes?" Melissa said with a laugh. "Maybe he'll faint and you can do a report on first aid at the same time."

Kenny, who always worried about other people's feelings, asked, "Do you think Mrs. Merrin is afraid of snakes?"

"If she can face Jeffrey every day, I don't think she's afraid of anything," Melissa teased.

Jeffrey looked at the box with interest. "If you've really got a snake in there, your report is going to be totally coolsville."

Ben raised one eyebrow. "*Coolsville?* Jeffrey, sometimes you're really weird."

Whoops, Jeffrey thought. Coolsville. That wasn't something that he'd normally say. But it *was* something that Max would say. Max always said things like "coolsville" and "dig you the most." Max talked like people had in the 1950s, because that's when Max had lived. Now he was a ghost. He was the third-grade ghost, and Jeffrey had found him in his desk at school.

The trouble was, no one but Jeffrey could see Max. So naturally no one else believed that Max

5

existed. Finally, Jeffrey had stopped trying to convince his friends that he really knew a ghost. When the water fountain all by itself suddenly started squirting people in the face, or when Mrs. Merrin wanted to show a videotape about the moon but Bugs Bunny cartoons came on instead, Jeffrey just sat there and enjoyed the show. He knew it was the Max Show—the funniest classroom show ever.

When they got to school, Ben put the box on the back table by the sink. He stuck a giant Do Not Disturb sign on it. Everyone wanted to know what was inside, but Ben wouldn't tell. He made Jeffrey, Kenny, and Melissa promise not to tell, either. Finally, after lunch, it was Ben's turn to give his science report.

"Don't worry," said Jeffrey, who sat next to Ben. "I'll help you out if it starts to get boring."

Ben picked up his shoe box and his note cards. He walked to the front of the classroom. Then he wrote the word *snake* on the chalkboard in wavy, snakelike letters.

"The snake is in the scientific order of Serpents," Ben said. "And you'll find them in the class of Reptiles."

"Just like this class," Brian Carr called out. Brian never really listened to anything

6

that was going on. And he always interrupted everyone.

Ben ignored him. "Just imagine for a moment that you are a snake," Ben said to the class. "How would you like to crawl on your stomach?"

"How'd you like to make me?" Brian demanded.

"That's enough, Brian," warned Mrs. Merrin.

"People don't understand a lot of things about snakes," Ben continued. "But now it's time to come face-to-face with the truth about snakes." With that, Ben dramatically ripped off the top of the shoe box. He pulled out Miranda, his long, dark garden snake. Miranda was a foot and a half long and thin. She curled around Ben's arm, her tongue darting in and out.

"Pass her around," said Melissa, who still wanted to get her hands on the snake.

"Don't do it!" shouted Arvin Pubbler. "Put it back in the box!"

Ben started to show the snake around. But Arvin kept yelling.

"It's on me! I can feel it!" Arvin yelled out.

Everyone looked over at him.

"It's crawling on my neck!" he said, afraid to move.

No one could see a snake on Arvin. And no one could understand why he was so upset. Only Jeffrey knew.

Standing next to Arvin was Max, the third-grade ghost. He was running his finger up and down Arvin Pubbler's back, giving him the chills. He made himself visible to Jeffrey for just a second. Then he disappeared again.

"Arvin," said Mrs. Merrin, trying to comfort her frightened student, "it's just your imagination."

No it's not, Jeffrey thought. But he kept the truth to himself.

Finally, Ben finished his report and put his snake back in the shoe box. Then he returned to his seat.

"I thought you were going to help me out," Ben whispered to Jeffrey.

"With Arvin screaming and Brian interrupting, it never got boring," Jeffrey replied.

"All right, class. Let's take out our writing journals," Mrs. Merrin said. She erased the word *snake* from the blackboard.

"It's not fair," Brian Carr blurted out. He said that about sixteen times a day.

"What's not fair this time, Brian?" asked the teacher.

"Ben gets to bring his pet to school," said Brian. "I want to bring my dog to school, too."

Mrs. Merrin smiled. "Ben's report was on snakes. What's your report on, Brian?"

"Electricity," answered Brian, "but—"

"But it would be really totally cool if we could bring our pets to class," said Connie Fazio.

Mrs. Merrin was quiet. She just let the students say what was on their minds. And everyone had something to say.

"Mrs. Merrin," said Melissa, "I'd like to bring my cat to school."

Ricky Reyes tapped Melissa on the shoulder. "Why don't you bring your snake instead?"

"I don't have a snake," Melissa said.

"Sure you do," Ricky said. "His name is Gary."

Ricky, Ben, and Melissa laughed. Ricky was right: Melissa's older brother, Gary, *was* a snake.

"Could we talk about something else besides pets?" Jeffrey said loudly.

But he was cut off by Becky Singer. "Mrs. Merrin, may I say something?" Becky was Melissa's best friend. She sat in the front of the class, so there was no way Mrs. Merrin could miss her raised hand. But when she got excited, Becky

10

had to call out. "I would just like to say—and I hope it doesn't hurt your feelings—if Ben brings his pet to school and we can't, I think that stinks."

When she heard that, Mrs. Merrin just stared at the class for a minute. Then she walked out of the room without saying anything.

"Uh-oh," Melissa said. "We pushed her too far that time."

Jeffrey nodded and waited with everyone else for Mrs. Merrin to return. A few minutes later she came back and sat down on the corner of her desk.

"Okay, guys, I've just been to the principal's office," she said. Everyone was very quiet. "And I'm happy to say, he's given us permission to have a Pet Day! So, how about this? Two weeks from today, everyone can bring in one pet for sharing."

The class cheered and applauded. Everyone except one person. Jeffrey Becker sat at his desk, resting his chin on his hands. "It's a terrible idea," he said. "I hate it."

Chapter Two

Jeffrey's bad mood did not improve when he walked home with his friends after school. How could it? Melissa, Ben, Kenny, and Ricky Reyes talked about Pet Day the whole way home. They all had pets. Jeffrey didn't.

"I've got to get my pet in shape," Ricky said. "And there're only two weeks to do it."

Ricky Reyes was one of the coolest and toughest kids in the third grade. He also knew karate. He had just recently become friends with Jeffrey, so there were still a lot of things Jeffrey didn't know about him.

"What kind of pet do you have, Ricky?" asked Melissa. She was walking backward all the way home.

"I'll bet you've got a Doberman," Kenny said.

"Or a vicuna," Ben said. He wasn't sure if anyone could really have one of those unless they lived in the Andes, but he liked saying it.

"I've got a frog," answered Ricky.

"A frog?" Ben said, laughing. It didn't seem like a Ricky Reyes kind of pet.

"Don't laugh," said Ricky. "He's a tough frog. I'm teaching him to attack. Eiiiyaah!" Ricky aimed a karate kick into the air.

"Well, I'll bring my dog to school," Kenny told them.

"That's nothing new," Ben said. "Your dog follows you to school at least twice a week."

"Hey, he's a really smart dog. He figured out how to open the backyard gate," Kenny said. "And I think he's learning to ride my bike."

Melissa groaned. "Come on, dogs can't ride bikes."

"No, I mean it," Kenny said. "Every day my bike's always in a different place from where I left it."

"Face it, Kenny, your little sister rides it before you get home from school," Ben said.

"No way," Kenny said positively. "I told her, 'Hands off my bike,' and I meant it. I'm sure it's my dog."

"I'm going to bring Furball on Pet Day," Melissa said. She was referring to her long-haired calico cat.

"Hey, Jeffrey," Ben said. He suddenly noticed that Jeffrey hadn't said a word the whole way home. "What's the matter?"

"Can we talk about something else besides pets?" Jeffrey asked. He kept walking, but his friends all stopped. They were quiet for a moment. Then they realized why Jeffrey was so upset, and they rushed to catch up with him.

"Jeffrey, I'm sorry," Melissa said. "We totally forgot about your parents' no-pets, not-now, not-ever, no-kidding policy."

"Yeah, after all, it's not normal. Only one kid in forty-eight doesn't have a pet," Ben said.

"Save the statistics for later, okay, Ben?" said Ricky.

"Sorry," Ben replied.

"Ben's right," Jeffrey said. "I'm a kid without a pet. I'm an oddball, a freak, a weirdo."

"We've been saying that for years," Ben teased with a smile.

"Well, that's all going to change," said Jeffrey. He was never without a plan for very long.

"What will you do?" Melissa asked.

"I'm going to ask my parents for a pet," Jeffrey announced.

"Wouldn't it be easier just to get new parents?" Kenny asked quietly. "Your mom can't

14

stand anything messy. And your dad starts sneezing if you just spell the word *dog*."

Jeffrey shrugged. "I've got two weeks to convince them to let me have a pet. That's plenty of time."

Jeffrey's attitude made his friends feel better, even if they didn't believe that his plan would work. By that time they had reached Kenny's house. He invited them inside to play Monopoly. But first he showed them that his bike was not where he had left it—positive proof that his dog had taken it for another joyride.

"What kind of pet are you going to get, Jeffrey?" Kenny asked during the Monopoly game. He moved his token around the board and landed on Water Works.

"I haven't decided yet," Jeffrey said. "Are you going to buy that, Kenny?"

"I don't think so," Kenny answered. "I bought it last time and then you said you were going to sue me because the water was polluted and made everyone sick. To settle out of court, I had to sell all my property and give you the money."

"Yeah, I wish you'd just stick to the rules, Becker," Ricky said to Jeffrey.

"Guys, I know for a fact that that's one of the

rules in the new version of the game that's coming out later this year," Jeffrey said.

Just then, Jeffrey was pounced on and nearly smothered by eighty pounds of quivering flesh and smelly fur. It was Kenny's Saint Bernard. Hotels, houses, and Monopoly money flew everywhere.

"Kenny, call off your dog!" Jeffrey said. The dog was squashing him.

"Max, get down," Kenny ordered his dog, but not in a very take-charge kind of voice. "He's just being friendly, Jeffrey. That's all."

Max began to lick Jeffrey's face. His tongue was so wet and sloppy, it felt like a sponge.

"He's not being friendly," Jeffrey said, from under the dog. "He thinks I'm an ice cream cone! Beat it, Max!"

"Hey! What's shaking, Daddy-o," said another Max. It was Max the ghost. "Like, how can I split the scene when I just arrived?"

"Not you—the dog!" Jeffrey told him.

"I know you're talking to the dog," Melissa said. "My name's not Max."

No one else in the room could see or hear the ghost. So they thought Jeffrey was talking to them.

16

Finally, Jeffrey got the dog to stop licking him and move away.

"Daddy-o, like, you're not going to need a bath for a month." Max stood there, invisible to everyone but Jeffrey. He was wearing his usual clothes from the 1950s. The cuffs of his baggy blue jeans were rolled up. And his hair was greased back, except for one dark curl that came over his forehead. But instead of the plaid flannel shirt he usually wore, he was wearing a bright polo shirt—Jeffrey's brand-new polo shirt.

"Hey, my shirt!" Jeffrey shouted.

"It's only got a little dog slobber on it," Kenny said.

"Like, I was just taking your shirt for a test drive," Max said. "Daddy-o, this scene is so squaresville I could put it in a box. Let's dig some sounds."

Max floated over and turned on the radio. He found a station playing rock 'n' roll from the fifties.

"Hey, who turned on the radio?" Melissa asked as she tried to straighten up the Monopoly board.

Kenny looked over at his radio. His dog was

17

sitting beside it, panting. "I don't believe it. Max turned it on!" Kenny exclaimed excitedly.

"Like, nobody else," said Max the ghost to Jeffrey.

"Well, I don't believe it, either," Ben said without much interest. "So tell him to turn it off and let's play the game."

"Max," Kenny said confidently to his giant dog. "Turn off the music, please."

And then everyone stared in surprise as the dog lifted his right front paw and turned off the radio.

"I don't believe it!" Melissa said.

"He really did it!" said Ricky Reyes.

Of course, what they couldn't see was Max the ghost. He had lifted the dog's paw in the air and then turned the radio off himself.

"I told you guys," Kenny said proudly. "My dog's not as dumb as he looks."

"Can we just play the game?" Jeffrey said.

He picked up the dice and rolled a three. But before Jeffrey could stop him, Max the ghost reached out and flipped the dice over until they both showed six on top.

"Hey, what happened to those dice?" Ricky asked. "First they said three and then twelve."

"Uh, haven't you ever heard of rolling doubles?" Jeffrey said nervously.

"Never mind the jokes, Becker, just roll the dice," Ricky said.

Jeffrey glared at his invisible friend. "Max, this time, leave the dice alone."

"Hey, don't blame my dog," Kenny said. "He's sitting on the other side of the room."

"I didn't mean your dog," Jeffrey said.

"How many Maxes are here?" Melissa asked.

"Don't forget Jeffrey's imaginary-ghost friend," Ben said sarcastically. "His name is Max, too."

Everyone except Jeffrey laughed. He rolled his eyes, then rolled the dice again. This time they didn't stop rolling for a full minute. When they finally stopped, it was twelve again—the number Jeffrey needed to pass Go.

The ghost laughed as he floated in the air above the Monopoly board. "Daddy-o, never fear. Like, you can't lose when Max is here."

"Okay, that's it," Ben said. "I'm not playing with a cheater."

"It wasn't me. It was Max," Jeffrey protested.

The dog, hearing his name, thought he was being called and launched himself at Jeffrey

again. This time he not only flattened Jeffrey, but he bent the Monopoly board, too.

The game was more than over—it was hopeless. Besides that, it was late. Time for everyone to go home. Melissa, Ricky, and Ben left quickly. But Jeffrey hung around to help Kenny put the game away.

"So, is Max going home with you?" Kenny asked.

"Are you kidding?" Jeffrey said. "I don't want to see your dog again till I've gained about forty pounds. If he jumps on me once more, you'll need a vacuum cleaner to get me out of your rug."

"I'm not talking about my dog," Kenny said. He stared at Jeffrey with a look that Jeffrey had never seen before. It was a look that said only one thing. Kenny knew there really was a ghost in the room!

Chapter Three

"Max, are you sure no one else can see you?" Jeffrey asked as he and his friend walked home from Kenny's house.

"Daddy-o, everyone can see me," said the ghost. "But it's like, I'm too wonderful for cats to dig. So their minds tell their eyes, 'No, no, no. Like, this can't be.' And that's why they don't believe what they see."

"I think Kenny knew you were there," Jeffrey told him.

"Groovy," said the ghost. "Like, make new friends but dig the old. Like, one is silver and one is mold."

"I think that's supposed to be gold, Max," Jeffrey said.

"I'm a poet and I know it," said Max. "What do you say we go home and dig the Larry, Curly, and Moe scene on your TV?"

"I can't. I've got to talk my parents into buying me a pet. That could take a few years."

"Parents are such squares they're practically cubes," said Max. "See you later, alligator." That was always Max's sign-off before he disappeared.

Mr. and Mrs. Becker were in the kitchen making dinner when Jeffrey got home.

"Hi, guys," Jeffrey said. "I've got news."

"Small news, medium news, or big news?" asked Mr. Becker. He was chopping vegetables for a salad.

"Well, it's good news and bad news," said Jeffrey. "The school psychologist says that I have extreme deframed psycho-hemo-dicosis."

"Is that the good news or the bad?" asked his mother, biting into a raw green bean.

"And the only way to cure it is for me to get a pet," Jeffrey went on.

"That's definitely the bad news," replied Jeffrey's father.

"Jeffrey, you know I don't like any animals with fur, scales, or skin," said Mrs. Becker.

"What if I find a pet that doesn't have those?" asked Jeffrey.

"I suggest you bury it quickly," his father said with a laugh he couldn't hold back.

"Very funny, Dad," said Jeffrey. He sat down glumly on a tall wooden kitchen stool. "Don't you want me to get over my extreme deframed psycho-hemo-dicosis?"

"Yes, almost as much as I'd like to hear you say it ten times real fast," said Mr. Becker.

His mother sighed. "Jeffrey, I'm sorry, but we just can't allow you to have a pet."

"Sure we can," said Mr. Becker.

Mrs. Becker stared at her husband. "We can?"

"If we don't, you know what's going to happen, don't you? Jeffrey will use all of his energy thinking of ways to get us to say yes. He won't straighten his room. He won't do his homework. He won't take out the garbage. And we won't get any sleep, any peace, or any younger."

"Go for it, Dad!" Jeffrey shouted.

"In short, life around here as we know it will come to a grinding halt," said Mr. Becker. "So now what do you say?"

Mrs. Becker looked from her husband to her son. "I say you *both* have extreme deframed psycho-hemo-dicosis!"

However, that weekend Mrs. Becker drove Jeffrey to the mall. They went into the pet store—just to look.

"May I help you?" asked the manager of the store. He was a friendly, bald man who never seemed to go anywhere without a large

24

spider on his shirt and a fluffy white bird on his head.

"You look like *you* need help," said Mrs. Becker when she noticed the spider.

"Mom, cool out," Jeffrey said. "You're acting like a grown-up, not a pet owner." He turned to the manager. "We'd like to see some pets."

"You've come to the right place," said the manager.

"Something small," Mrs. Becker told him.

"How small?" the manager asked.

"Do you have anything so small you have to look at it under a microscope?" she asked.

The manager scowled and looked at Mrs. Becker as if *she* were a germ.

"How about a cat?" Jeffrey asked. "They're good pets, aren't they?"

"Yes," said the manager.

"No," said Mrs. Becker. "They're too sneaky." She shook her head and gave Jeffrey her I-mean-business glare.

"Well, then, a dog," said Jeffrey.

"Sure," said the pet-store manager.

"No," said Mrs. Becker.

Jeffrey shook his head. "Mom, after cats and dogs come gorillas and rhinos."

"Okay, maybe a dog," said Mrs. Becker.

25

"Something small with a wind-up key on the side would be best."

"First-time pet owner, huh?" asked the store manager.

"How can you tell?" Mrs. Becker asked nervously.

"Maybe we'd better just look around by ourselves," Jeffrey suggested.

As Jeffrey and his mom walked around the pet shop, Jeffrey pointed out the dogs that he liked. But Mrs. Becker found something wrong with each of them. She criticized everything from the length of their fur to the length of their tails to the length of their names.

"How about this one, Mom?"

"That dog's a born menace, a killer," said Mrs. Becker. "I don't like the way he's looking at you."

"But, Mom! He's not looking at me. He's asleep," said Jeffrey. He reached into the cage and petted the cuddly little cocker spaniel inside. Then they moved to the next cage. "How about this one?" Jeffrey asked. He was pointing to a sad-eyed, golden-colored dog.

"Uh-uh. He's bigger than you are and he probably eats five times as much," said Mrs. Becker.

"You're wrong there, Mom. This is a special new breed that grows to fit its environment," Jeffrey explained. "If you keep him in the house, he shrinks down to the size of a throw pillow. Honest."

"Jeffrey," said Mrs. Becker, "don't take this the wrong way, but this place is giving me the creeps. If I don't get out of here soon, I'll break out in hives."

"Maybe I should get some bees, then, huh, Mom?"

"Jeffrey, how about this for a plan. You look around the pet shop while I go into the mall to do some shopping. Then in half an hour, I'll meet you at the benches outside."

"Deal, Mom," Jeffrey said.

Mrs. Becker left, and Jeffrey walked through the store. In one cage he saw three shepherd puppies chasing each other. In the next cage, two tiny dachshunds slept side by side.

"What's shaking, Daddy-o?" said a voice behind Jeffrey.

Jeffrey turned around and saw Max. He was wearing the bright red sweatband and wristbands that Jeffrey had given him for Christmas.

"Great outfit, Max," Jeffrey said, smiling. "But you won't believe what happened."

"Like, your folks said coolsville to you buying a pet, right?" guessed the ghost.

"How did you know that?" Jeffrey asked.

"Daddy-o, who do you think invented extreme deframed psycho-hemo-dicosis? I used to get it twice a week when I was coming at you live and in living color."

Jeffrey laughed. Max always claimed to have invented the stuff that Jeffrey thought up. "Let's check out that big Old English sheepdog, Max. If I'm going to get a dog, I want it to be as big and hairy as possible."

Jeffrey walked over to the sheepdog and it started wagging its tail. But then the dog saw Max. Suddenly its lips curled back, showing gleaming white teeth. The dog growled for a moment, then started barking.

"Mistakesville, Daddy-o," said Max. "I forgot that dogs and cats can see me! And they don't dig a cat like me from ghostville."

"Oh, no," Jeffrey moaned. "That's terrible!"

"Hey, stop bothering the animals," the manager called to Jeffrey.

Jeffrey and Max moved away quickly from the sheepdog. But everywhere they moved, more dogs started barking. Cats arched their backs and hissed.

"I don't get it," Jeffrey said. "Why didn't Kenny's dog, Max, go nuts when he saw you the other day?"

Max shrugged. "That dog is so dumbsville, he wouldn't even chase a cat." The ghost looked around the pet store. "Daddy-o, I don't think this is my scene."

All of the animals in the store were going wild. They had changed from sweet pets to total monsters because they knew, sensed, or saw that a ghost was there.

"You expect me to buy this kitten for my granddaughter?" complained a gray-haired woman to the manager. "Never in a million years!" The kitten she was holding had dug its claws into her sleeve and wouldn't let go. It was hissing at Max.

Soon, all of the customers left the store. But the dogs and cats kept jumping around. They were spilling their water and food. The birds flew back and forth in their cages.

"This place is a zoo," Max said, holding his ears. "See you later, alligator." Then he instantly disappeared.

"Alligator? Maybe that's what I should get," Jeffrey said unhappily. He realized that he couldn't get a dog or a cat. Not if he wanted to have a ghost for a friend.

Of course, the store manager couldn't see Max at all. He thought the animals were barking and hissing because of something Jeffrey had done.

"Out," the manager ordered, glaring angrily at Jeffrey. "You've caused enough trouble for one day."

So Jeffrey left the pet store—without Max and without a pet.

"Jeffrey," said his mother when he met her at the benches. "I've made a decision. You can have a dog. It's what you want and it's what you should have."

"Are you kidding, Mom?" Jeffrey said. He looked at the pet store and thought of Max. "A dog is the last thing in the world I want!"

Chapter Four

"Jeffrey, I've got to talk to you," said Kenny Thompsen, the next day at school. He sat down next to Jeffrey.

"I'm kinda busy," Jeffrey told him. Jeffrey was in the reading section of the classroom. He had stayed inside during recess because it was February 14, Valentine's Day. On Valentine's Day, Jeffrey always stayed away from the playground. It had been a rule of his ever since the first grade when Carolyn Moss tried to kiss him on the mouth.

"Jeffrey," said Kenny, "you've been 'kinda busy' a lot lately. Like, every time I want to talk to you about the ghost."

Jeffrey looked at Kenny. "Hey, you got a haircut yesterday!" he said, changing the subject.

"And you've been changing the subject a lot, too," Kenny said. "Jeffrey, for months you've been trying to get us to believe that you knew a ghost. Now that I do, you know what I think?

32

I think you want to keep the ghost all to yourself. But I know there's a ghost and I have the proof."

The two friends stared at each other. Kenny's eyes were twinkling like sparklers. He held out a small stack of valentines. "Read these," Kenny said.

Jeffrey read the first two cards.

Roses are red, prunes are stewed,
I think you are one cool dude.

Signed,
A Secret Admirer

If I'll be your arrow, will you be my beau?

Signed,
A Secret Admirer

"I've found these cards everywhere today," Kenny said. "In my desk, in my books, in my jacket, in my lunch, taped to my locker. I even found a trail of them coming out of my house."

Jeffrey smiled. "Some girl is really after you. But what does that have to do with Max? Where's your proof that my ghost exists?" Jeffrey asked.

"That's my proof," Kenny said. "The valentines."

Just then, Melissa came back from recess. "Hi, guys. What's happening?" she asked.

"Kenny has a secret admirer," Jeffrey said.

"Oh, really." Melissa winked at Jeffrey. "Who is it, Kenny?"

"You think I won't tell or something, don't

you, Jeffrey?" Kenny said. Then he turned to Melissa. "It's Max," Kenny told her.

Melissa almost lost it at that point. "Your *dog*?" she screamed. "Are you totally bananas?"

"Not my dog," Kenny said. "Max the ghost. There really is a ghost, isn't there, Jeffrey?"

Jeffrey squirmed a little. But Melissa kept talking.

"A ghost? Forget it, Kenny. Don't try to act as crazy as Jeffrey. It's not possible," Melissa said. "For your information, I know who those cards are from. And I'd tell you if I hadn't promised someone that I wouldn't. So you can ask me as many times as you want, but I'll never tell you that Becky Singer sent you those cards."

Kenny didn't say anything—or even move— for a moment. Then he slowly turned his head to look at Becky Singer.

Becky's blond curls didn't look anything like Melissa's long red ponytail. And Becky wasn't athletic like Melissa. But still, Becky and Melissa were perfect best friends. They both liked things to be organized a certain way—their way.

"You mean a *girl* sent these to me?" Kenny said.

Melissa rolled her eyes. "You dodo brain. Becky likes you."

Kenny's expression changed from excitement to disappointment. "This isn't fair," he said. "I thought I was getting cards from a ghost. And it turns out they're from a girl. Now what do I do?"

"You go over and say something nice to her," Melissa said. "She spent a bundle on cards for you."

"Are you nuts?" Kenny asked. "I can't thank her for these things. There are *hearts* all over them!"

"Kenny." Jeffrey put his arm around his friend's neck. "You've got to learn the right way to deal with girls. Go over there and tell her how far you can spit. Then ask her if she wants to see you do it."

Melissa gave Jeffrey a punch on the arm. "Ask her what she thinks of your new haircut," Melissa said. "That will keep Becky happy through lunchtime."

"You guys are no help at all," Kenny said.

Melissa and Jeffrey watched Kenny walk slowly over to Becky's desk. Then he quickly changed his mind and walked the other way.

"Does Becky still want to marry Kenny?" Jeffrey asked.

"Yeah, but she's willing to wait till fifth grade," Melissa said.

Jeffrey shook his head and went back to his desk. He opened the lid to put his notebook away. Inside, there was a red envelope resting on top of his books. It hadn't been there before. On the front, in crayon, it said, "Daddy-o." Jeffrey knew right away who his secret admirer was. And wouldn't Kenny die if he saw it?

Jeffrey opened the envelope. Written on the front of the card was, "Valentine, like, my heart bleeds for you." When Jeffrey opened it, red catsup dripped onto his pants. It was the perfect Max valentine—never what Jeffrey expected and always a surprise.

That afternoon when Jeffrey got home, Max was waiting in his bedroom with a happy grin on his face. But he was hiding something behind his back. Jeffrey knew by now that that meant only one thing: Trouble was on its way.

"Thanks for your card, Max," Jeffrey said. "It really *dripped* with good feelings."

"Well, it's presentsville for you, one more time," said Max. Then he brought his hands forward. "Here's your new pet, Daddy-o."

Jeffrey couldn't believe his eyes. Max was holding a large, long, brown-spotted lizard! It was great! The lizard was about two feet long and weighed almost thirty pounds. It flicked its long pink tongue out at Jeffrey.

"His name is Elvis, but, like, you can just call him the King," said Max. He held the lizard out to Jeffrey.

"Wow, Max," Jeffrey said, petting the lizard. "He's awesome. Where did you get him?"

"What difference does it make?" Max said. "Like, the King is here just in the nicksville for Pet Day. You're going to love him."

"Boy, what a great pet for Pet Day," Jeffrey said. "Everyone will be bragging, 'My pet is bigger than your pet.' And I'll just tell them, 'So what . . . my pet just ate your pet.' "

"Like, there are two little things you have to remember about the King," Max said. "You've got to keep your room groovy and hot."

"Hot? How hot?"

"I think about one hundred and ten degrees should do it," the ghost said, petting the squirming lizard.

"A hundred and ten degrees—that's like a desert!" Jeffrey said.

"That's the other little thing," said Max. "Like, you've got to fill your pad with sand. That's what the King digs the most."

All of a sudden Elvis twisted and wriggled in

Max's hands. He was so strong and so fast that
he squirmed away. He ran over Jeffrey's
dresser, knocking everything onto the floor.

Then he jumped from the dresser to the rug and kept running.

"Quick, Max! Close the door."

Both boys chased the lizard around Jeffrey's bedroom. They crashed into Jeffrey's desk and knocked over lamps and chairs. But Elvis remained free.

"I can't find him," Jeffrey said, looking under his bed. "He's the same color as my rug."

Just then, the door to Jeffrey's room opened. Mrs. Becker stood there looking at her son—and at the mess in his room.

"Jeffrey, what are you doing?" she asked.

"Uh, ballet, Mom," Jeffrey said, clearing his throat.

"You don't take ballet," his confused mother replied.

"I was going to surprise you," Jeffrey said. "I've been working on my triple."

"Triple what?"

"Uh, well, that's where the surprise comes in," said Jeffrey. "Mom, would you mind closing my door?"

"My pleasure," said Mrs. Becker softly. As she left the room, her face had a funny look on it. It was a look that meant she wondered if Jeffrey might be from another planet.

"Like, gotcha!" Max said, holding up the squirming prize he had captured under Jeffrey's bed. It was Elvis.

Jeffrey was beginning to think that Elvis was too hard to handle. "Max," he said. "Elvis is a great lizard, but maybe he's not such a great pet."

"Like, he'd keep you in shape, Daddy-o," said Max.

"And he'd help me redecorate my room, too," Jeffrey said. "Please, Max, take Elvis back to where you got him."

"No sweat," said the ghost.

"Thanks," said Jeffrey.

"It's cool. Like, I've still got a groovy shopping list," said Max. "See you later, alligator."

"Shopping list?" Jeffrey said. But it was too late. Max was gone. "Oh, no," Jeffrey moaned. "What is he going to bring me next time?"

Chapter Five

Pet Day came closer and closer. And every day that week Max brought Jeffrey a different animal to try out as a pet. Jeffrey liked Max's Try-a-Pet Plan. But he also worried about it. Where was Max getting all of the animals?

After Elvis, Max brought a rabbit—a fat brown rabbit. It was so fat, it could hardly move. The animal hopped slowly around Jeffrey's bedroom. "I'll bet the tortoise would like a rematch with this guy," Jeffrey said.

"Daddy-o," Max said, "like, this is one special nose twitcher."

"Why? Does it talk?" asked Jeffrey.

Max shook his head. "That would be bad news. Guess again."

"He has his own credit cards?" Jeffrey said.

"Never mind," said Max. "All you have to know is he is one great bunny. Trust me."

While the two friends talked, the bunny was doing what bunnies do best. He was making a mess all over Jeffrey's rug. And Jeffrey didn't like that one bit.

"Max, this rabbit is ruining my room," Jeffrey said.

"Daddy-o," said the ghost, "it's a big room. You two can take turns."

But when Jeffrey came home from school the next day, the rabbit was gone. Instead, there were two yellow parakeets in a small wire cage. They were smaller than the rabbit, but they were even messier.

Every time they tried to fly in their cage or just flapped their wings, feathers and bird seeds flew everywhere. Jeffrey had to get the vacuum cleaner to clean up the mess each time it happened. He had to vacuum eight times that day.

To make matters worse, the birds were as noisy as they were messy. They chirped and chattered nonstop until it was dark. Then, as soon as the sun came up the next morning, the birds started to sing again.

Mr. Becker opened Jeffrey's door and poked his sleepy face inside.

"Jeffrey, you have birds in your room," he said.

"Right as usual, Dad," Jeffrey called. He was lying in bed with his pillow covering his head.

Mr. Becker sat down on Jeffrey's bed and yawned. "Why do you have birds in your room?" he asked.

Jeffrey sat up. "Uh, gee, Dad, I thought you knew. I think you're going to be proud of me. I've joined a new club," he said. "It's the endangered species club. They send me a different animal every week to nurse and take care of."

"But those birds are parakeets," said Mr. Becker. "Parakeets are not an endangered species—although these two may be if they don't shut up."

"Dad, these aren't parakeets. They're bald eagles," Jeffrey explained.

"They look like parakeets to me," said Mr. Becker.

"They're bald eagles. But they're in disguise so that no one will recognize them," Jeffrey said.

Mr. Becker nodded. "I guess I'm just sleepy enough to believe you," he said. He stood up to walk out of the room. "And throw a cover over their cage so that we can get some sleep."

That afternoon Max's pet express stopped in Jeffrey's room once again. This time Max left a large green turtle. It was about the size of an

44

alarm clock. It came in a tank filled with shallow water.

The only problem was, the turtle wouldn't come out of its shell. At first Jeffrey thought it was just getting used to its new home. But when Jeffrey checked on the turtle after dinner, it still hadn't moved. Not an inch.

"Well, I've already taught it one trick," Jeffrey said. "Play dead!"

And the turtle didn't move a bit.

After a while Jeffrey tried to think of ways to get the turtle to come out. "Fire! Fire! Run for your life!" he shouted.

Mr. Becker burst into Jeffrey's room. He was carrying a small fire extinguisher. Jeffrey's father looked around. He smelled no smoke. He saw no flames. All he saw was Jeffrey on his knees staring at a turtle.

"Jeffrey," Mr. Becker said sternly, "don't you know about the boy who shouted fire?"

"I thought that was wolf, Dad," said Jeffrey.

"Be on the safe side and don't shout anything, okay?" said his father. "What happened to the bald eagles?"

"I got them wigs," Jeffrey said. "It improved their confidence so much, they flew away."

"Good for you," Mr. Becker replied. Then he looked at Jeffrey's new turtle. It still wasn't moving at all. "Looks like your turtle flew south for the winter with the birds. Are you sure he's in there?"

"Oh, sure, Dad," Jeffrey said. "He's just taking a break. I was playing fetch with him before you came up. When he gets going he's just a blur."

"Jeffrey, you definitely have a way with animals. And it's almost as good as your way with words," Mr. Becker said with a smile.

After his father left, Jeffrey sat glumly on his bed. The turtle still hadn't moved. I might as well just have a photograph of a turtle, Jeffrey thought. This turtle's got to go.

And it did. Butch, the goldfish, moved in the next day. When Jeffrey got home from school, he found a fish tank. It was filled with tubes and filters and ceramic divers and green seaweed and plastic glittery starfish. There was so much stuff that Jeffrey couldn't see the goldfish. And, in fact, Max had been so busy putting things in the tank, he had forgotten to include a goldfish.

"Max," said Jeffrey, "what I want is a pet that I can put a leash on. I want to teach it tricks and have it sleep on my bed and feed it my brussels sprouts under the table."

"Like, I am totally hip to what you mean," said the ghost.

The next day Max showed up with a hamster.

"Max, I can't put a leash on him or teach him tricks or any of that other stuff. He's too small."

"Jeffrey, dig this: He's not done growing. Like, give him some timesville."

Jeffrey watched the little brown hamster in his cage. He was running like a nut on a small exercise wheel.

"Where are you getting these animals, Max?" asked Jeffrey.

But, as usual, Max wouldn't answer. He just disappeared.

Jeffrey opened the hamster's cage. Maybe this *is* the pet for me, he thought—until the hamster bit him on the hand. Jeffrey pulled his hand out quickly and closed the cage.

"Great," he mumbled. "Max said be sure to feed him. But he forgot to say feed him with my hand."

After that, every time Jeffrey tried to pick up the hamster or to change his food and water, the hamster would squeal and bite Jeffrey as hard as he could. Jeffrey couldn't wait for Max to return.

"Like, how did you and your little buddy get along?" asked Max the next afternoon.

"If tomorrow were Bruises and Wounds Day instead of Pet Day, I'd be in great shape," Jeffrey said. He showed Max the Band-Aids on his hand. "First you bring a rabbit that's totally messy. Then birds with too much personality and a turtle with no personality at all. The goldfish was invisible and the hamster hates me. I think we have to face the fact that this isn't working out."

Then with a jazzy "Ta-Da!" Max unveiled his latest and greatest pet. It was a large white bird that looked at Jeffrey with unblinking black eyes.

"Coolsville, Daddy-o," the bird said.

"Wow!" Jeffrey exclaimed.

"What's shaking, Daddy-o?" said the bird.

"Like, he's a quick learner," said Max, putting the bird on Jeffrey's shoulder.

"Max, he's great!" said Jeffrey. "You've done it! You've found the perfect pet! Can I keep him?"

"Like, yeah," said the ghost. "And he's even

cooler than a little brother because he'll only
say what you tell him to say."

When Jeffrey went down to dinner that night,
the bird was still on his shoulder.

Jeffrey's parents were getting used to seeing animals crawling or clinging to Jeffrey. But they were still surprised to see the big white bird.

"Where on earth did you get that thing?" Mrs. Becker said, moving around the table away from Jeffrey.

"It comes from a country where there's a hot climate and not much roller skating," Jeffrey said. He was trying to answer her without really answering her. "His name is Alonzo. Say hello, Alonzo."

"What's shaking, Daddy-o?" said the bird. "Coolsville, coolsville!"

"He must be from a faraway country. He's definitely speaking a foreign language," Mr. Becker said with a laugh.

"You know, I think I've seen that bird somewhere before," said Mrs. Becker. "Well, sit down and let's eat. We're having your favorite, Jeffrey. Fried chicken."

"*Please*, Mom. Not so loud," Jeffrey said. He used his thumb to point up at the bird on his shoulder. "It was just a joke, Alonzo. We'd never eat a bird."

"Squaresville," said the bird.

"Jeffrey, would you pass the *chick* peas, please," said Mrs. Becker with a laugh.

"Ha ha," Jeffrey said.

"May I help you?" said Alonzo. "May I help you?"

Jeffrey and his mother stared at each other.

"Jeffrey, I just remembered where I saw this bird," said Mrs. Becker.

But Jeffrey had just remembered, too. It was the same bird that had been sitting on the head of the pet-store manager at the mall!

Jeffrey's heart sank. Great, he thought to himself. I finally get a pet I really like and it belongs to someone else! Thanks for nothing, Max.

"Jeffrey, how much did that bird cost?" Mrs. Becker asked.

"Too much, Mom," Jeffrey said. "He's going back tomorrow."

Then he excused himself and rushed upstairs to his room. "Max," he said, "you always seem to hear me when I need you. Well, I need to see you *now*. I'm in big trouble and it's all because of y-o-u!"

The ghost appeared, flipping a yo-yo up and down, up and down.

"Max, have you been getting all of these animals from the pet store?"

"Hey, Daddy-o, you can't find 'em at the car wash," said Max.

"May I help you? Don't rattle the cages," said Alonzo.

"But you've been stealing them," Jeffrey said. "That's animal-napping!"

"Naah. Like, none of them were sleeping," said the ghost.

"Not that kind of *napping*," said Jeffrey. "I love Alonzo, but I can't keep him, Max. You'll have to take him back."

"Like, why? Was it something he said?" asked Max. He looked as if his feelings were hurt.

"Max, I know you're trying to help me. And you pick out animals better than anyone I know," Jeffrey said. "But it looks like I'm just going to have to go to Pet Day without a pet."

"What a drag," the bird squawked.

"Like, you can say that again," said Max.

And the bird did, several times.

Chapter Six

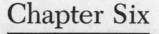

The next day was Pet Day. At breakfast, Jeffrey wasn't very hungry. He stared at his bowl of Critter Creatures cereal until the little green and orange toasted-oat animals turned soggy. The critters sank to the bottom. Meanwhile, all of the little black power balls, which were really marshmallows, floated to the top.

Okay, Jeffrey thought to himself. So most kids have pets. But I'll bet I'm the only kid who has a ghost for a friend.

Thinking about Max made Jeffrey think about Kenny Thompsen. Kenny's questions about Max were now nonstop. He was like a bloodhound hot on the trail of a ghost. Jeffrey wanted to answer Kenny's questions. And he *really* wanted Kenny to meet Max. But Max kept saying, "Like, don't rush me, Daddy-o."

"Jeff-free, Jeff-free!"

Outside on the front lawn, Melissa, Ben, and Kenny were calling Jeffrey's name. They were all excited because they had their pets with them. They were waiting for Jeffrey to walk to school.

Jeffrey went outside empty-handed.

"No pet, huh?" Melissa said. She had her cat, Furball, in a cat carrier with a domed plastic lid.

"I ordered a coyote by mail a week ago," Jeffrey explained. "I guess it got tied up in traffic."

"You can help me walk my dog," Kenny said. Kenny's Saint Bernard, Max, was much stronger than he. It dragged Kenny anywhere it wanted to go.

"It looks more like Max is taking *you* to school," Jeffrey said, laughing. "Guys, don't worry about me. I'm not upset about Pet Day. Honest. It's like a vacation."

"How come?" asked Ben. He was carrying his snake in an enormous wooden box. It was so big it had to be wheeled to school on his old wagon. Jeffrey wondered if Miranda had grown.

"Because with all of the animals in class, we won't do any schoolwork," Jeffrey explained. "So I didn't do any of my homework last night. Pet Day is great with me."

"Then let's pick up the pace and get there," Melissa said, walking faster.

The others followed.

When Jeffrey got to school, he was the only kid who didn't have a pet. He couldn't even get to his desk without walking around or stepping over all of the animals. There were dogs and cats and turtles and butterflies and fish and frogs and mice and gerbils and hamsters and spiders. Even Mrs. Merrin brought her black cocker spaniel puppy.

Jeffrey looked around. He was hoping to see Max. But Max was nowhere to be seen. A frog hopped off Jeffrey's chair just before he sat down.

When everyone had arrived with their pets, Ben opened the lid of his box. Miranda, the garden snake, was not inside. Instead, there was a huge, fat snake about five feet long!

"Oh, no!" Mrs. Merrin exclaimed when she saw the snake. "It's a boa constrictor!"

"I bet Brian will listen to my snake report *now*," said Ben with a big laugh.

The snake slithered slowly out of the box. It seemed to take forever to get from the box to the floor. The ceiling lights made the snake's body gleam.

Everyone grabbed their pets and stood back—far back.

"Ben!" said Mrs. Merrin, trying to sound as calm as possible. She held her puppy tightly in her arms. "Could you put your pet back in the box for now? It's looking hungrily at my desk."

"They like exercise," Ben said.

"*Now,* Ben," Mrs. Merrin said sternly.

Ben lifted the heavy boa constrictor and stuffed it back into its wooden box. Then he closed the lid.

With the snake tucked away, Mrs. Merrin put her puppy on the floor and started the day. "Good morning, everyone—and I do mean everyone." With all the barking, she had to raise her voice to be heard. "I want to welcome all of our friends to Pet Day. This is going to be a day to remember, I can tell."

As she talked, she walked around the classroom, and her little puppy followed. She petted the animals she could pet and looked at those that were in dishes, bowls, and tanks. "However, guys, we still have classwork to do."

That news set off an alarm in Jeffrey's head.

"So I want everyone to put their animals away for a while," Mrs. Merrin continued. "If you'll look around the room, you'll see we have three areas for the pets. This way we can keep the dogs away from the cats. And the cats will be away from the birds and the mice and the gerbils. And we probably should keep Ben's snake away from *everything!*"

One by one, the students took their cats to the coat closet area. The small animals went to the sink area. And the dogs went to the special dog area Mrs. Merrin had built in the reading center.

When everyone was back at their desks, Mrs. Merrin said, "So far, so good. Everyone's getting along fine. Now let's check our math homework. And to read his answers, I'm happy to call on Jeffrey Becker."

Math homework? Math homework? Jeffrey

said the two words over and over in his mind. They were the last two words he had expected to hear today. For a second he thought he should just tell her he didn't do it. But he got over that quickly.

"I know why you're calling on me, Mrs. Merrin," he said.

"So you can read your math homework," answered his teacher.

"I know you feel sorry for me since I'm the only kid here without a pet," Jeffrey said.

Mrs. Merrin shook her head.

"I know. You think I feel sad and left out and pitiful. And you think you can make it up to me by giving me a lot of special attention."

"Jeffrey—" the teacher started to say. But Jeffrey interrupted her.

"Well, forget it," he said. "Choosing me to read my math answers is the worst thing you can do. It could set me back years. It could bring on a case of extreme deframed psycho-hemodicosis!"

Mrs. Merrin's eyes opened wide.

"The best thing you can do is to pretend that I'm not here at all," Jeffrey said. As a final gesture, he buried his head in his arms on his desk and pretended to sob.

"Jeffrey," Mrs. Merrin said, walking over to him quietly. "I'm sorry that you don't have a pet. And I'm sorry that Pet Day won't be as much fun for you as it will for the rest of us. But mostly I'm very sorry that you didn't do your math homework last night. So be sure to do it over the weekend." She pulled on his ears playfully. "Extreme deframed psycho-hemo-dicosis, my foot."

Suddenly, the animals in the room became restless. The dogs whined and the cats hissed and Arvin Pubbler's rabbit started to thump.

"What's wrong with them?" Melissa asked.

"I think Jeffrey's bad acting scared them," Mrs. Merrin said, smiling.

Jeffrey smiled, too. He knew what was wrong with the animals—and he knew if he explained it, no one would believe him. Max the ghost was walking around the room. And the animals were freaking out.

Suddenly, Jeffrey noticed that Kenny was watching him. And Kenny had a smile on his face, too.

"The animals are getting restless, guys," Mrs. Merrin said. "So I think I'm going to change my plan. Let's start Pet Day right now."

Mrs. Merrin then called on the students in alphabetical order to show their pets.

Jenny Arthur was first. "I have a mouse," she said, giggling and standing up by her desk. "He's white and his name is Apple because I got him the same day we got our computer and it has a mouse, too. And I really like the way he climbs all over my neck. His claws tickle."

Then Jenny went to the sink area to bring back Apple's cage. A moment later Jeffrey heard her cry out. When she came back with the cage, the mouse wasn't in it.

"It's not funny, you guys," Jenny said. "Did someone open Apple's cage?"

No one had opened it. The rest of the class was sure of that and everyone said so.

"Apple's gone," Jenny said. She sounded and looked upset. "His cage was right next to . . . right next to . . ." She was having trouble finishing her sentence. "His cage was right next to *your* snake's box, Ben!" Jenny began to cry.

"Wait a minute, Jenny," Ben said.

"I think your horrible snake ate my mouse!"

Quickly, Mrs. Merrin came up and put her arm around Jenny. She tried to calm her down. But it didn't work. The mouse was gone and it looked as if the snake had eaten it.

Just then Kenny leaned over to Jeffrey. As if he could read Jeffrey's mind, he said what Jeffrey was thinking. "I know who took the mouse. Max did!"

"Your dog?" Jeffrey said.

"No," Kenny said firmly. "Your ghost!"

Chapter Seven

While Mrs. Merrin was comforting Jenny, Jeffrey pulled Kenny out into the hall.

"Look," Jeffrey said, "a mouse is missing. That's all. That's no reason to think there's a ghost in the room."

"I've thought about this a lot," Kenny said. "Weird things keep happening around you. And they're always the kinds of things a ghost would do. Besides, ever since last September you've been saying that you found a ghost at school. So I think your ghost stole Jenny Arthur's mouse."

Jeffrey didn't know what to say. Should he admit that Kenny was right about Max? And what would Max do if Kenny knew the truth? Would he show himself to Kenny? Or would he just disappear—for good?

"Let's talk about it later," Jeffrey said, walking quickly back into the room.

Jenny Arthur was still crying about Apple.

Mrs. Merrin wiped away her tears. "Why did you have to bring that snake today, anyway?" Jenny whined to Ben. "It ate Apple."

"My snake?" Ben said to Jenny. "No way. Why would my snake eat your puny little mouse when it could have its pick of any of these parakeets or cats?"

"Ben," said Mrs. Merrin, "that's not funny. And it's not going to make Jenny feel better."

"Maybe your mouse just got loose," Jeffrey said to Jenny.

Jenny shook her head. "He was in his cage and the door was locked," she said.

"I know," Jeffrey said. "Mice like to act dumb during the day when people are watching them. But it's been proven that at night they read the newspaper that's on the bottom of their cage."

Jenny looked at Jeffrey with half-believing eyes. Kenny was watching Jeffrey, too.

"Now what if you put the do-it-yourself home-repair section of the newspaper in his cage?" Jeffrey went on. "Don't you see? He probably figured out how to open the door by himself."

"He *is* really smart," said Jenny. "But if he got out, he's really dead. There must be five cats here. Apple doesn't stand a chance."

"He probably left the room," Jeffrey said.

"I've got a plan. Everyone else go on with Pet Day. I'll search the school, looking for Apple."

Mrs. Merrin shook her head. "No way, Jeffrey. I can't let you just go wandering around."

"But, Mrs. Merrin," Jeffrey pleaded in a phony voice. "I feel *useless* here. I'm the *only* kid without a pet, remember? And I promise I'll find her mouse and come right back."

Finally, Mrs. Merrin gave in and Jeffrey went out into the hall. He pretended to look for Apple. But secretly he thought that maybe Kenny was right. Maybe Max *had* taken the mouse. So his real plan was to look for Max!

But Kenny followed him into the hall. He was watching every move Jeffrey made.

"Jeffrey, is he here yet? What will he look like?" Kenny asked.

"He'll look like a little white mouse," Jeffrey said.

"Not the mouse. The ghost," Kenny said. He looked a little hurt. "I don't get why you've changed, Jeffrey. Why don't you admit that there's a ghost?"

Jeffrey thought about it for a minute. "Kenny, you don't really want to know about ghosts," he said at last. "Because no one would ever believe you. And every time you'd try to tell your best friends that you knew about something that was so totally cool, you know what they'd say? They'd say, 'Nice try, Kenny. Ha ha. Big joke.' "

"I'm sorry we teased you, Jeffrey," said Kenny. "Really."

Jeffrey smiled at his friend. "Thanks," he said.

"So, where's the ghost?" Kenny asked excitedly.

"What ghost?" said Jeffrey with a straight face.

"Okay. I give up," Kenny said. "Tell you what. I'll help you look for the mouse."

"Thanks," Jeffrey said. "You check the third floor and I'll check this one."

When Kenny was gone, Jeffrey tried to get Max to appear.

"Max," he called quietly. But Max was out of sight—and staying that way.

Five minutes later, Kenny came back. "Jeffrey," he said. "I think I saw the mouse! He went into a broom closet on the third floor."

Jeffrey followed his friend through the quiet halls of the school. They went up the stairs to the third floor.

When they reached the broom closet, Jeffrey asked, "Are you sure he went in here?"

"Jenny's going to be really happy that you found him," Kenny said, looking away. "You go first."

Jeffrey opened the door and walked into the closet. But as soon as he was inside, Kenny slammed the door shut!

Jeffrey was trapped!

He pounded on the door. But he knew it wouldn't open. This was the same closet that *he* had locked *Kenny* in once a long time ago. It was the perfect closet in which to lock people because there was no doorknob on the inside. It could only be opened from the outside.

Jeffrey had to get out of there. "Max!" he called. "Max! Help!" Jeffrey hoped the ghost could hear him. He called again.

Suddenly, the door opened slowly. At first, no one was there. Then, bit by bit, Max began to appear.

"What's shaking, Daddy-o?" asked the ghost. He was standing there, wearing a different shirt again. It was a white T-shirt with the sleeves rolled up to his shoulders. On the front of the shirt, painted in red paint, were the words Pet Day. "Pet Day's a gas," Max said. "I've never had a pet before."

"Is that why you took Jenny Arthur's mouse?" Jeffrey asked.

"No, Daddy-o," said Max.

"You mean you didn't take it?"

"Daddy-o, like, I *did* split with the mouse," Max said.

"Then you've got to give it back," Jeffrey said.

"Like, I don't think you'd dig it if I did," Max said. He put his hand in his pocket and pulled out Jenny's mouse.

Jeffrey was happy to see Apple, but only for a moment.

"Wait a minute," he said. "I can see right through the mouse . . . *the same way I can see through you.*"

"I'm hip, Daddy-o," said Max. "That's because this mouse took a one-way trip to ghostville."

"You mean Apple died?" Jeffrey asked sadly.

"Like, completely. Bad scene. Mice don't live forever," Max said.

The little ghost mouse sat happily in Max's hand.

"I eyeballed this little cheese-nibbler in his cage," Max said. "And I knew Jenny would flip out if she found him coldsville. So, like, I removed the evidence. He's kind of groovy in a fuzzy way."

"Oh, no," Jeffrey moaned. "How am I going to tell Jenny that her mouse is dead?"

Max reached into the other pocket of his jeans. He pulled out another white mouse. This one was very fat and very much alive. "Like, why tell her?" asked the ghost. "Meet the new, improved Apple, Daddy-o."

Jeffrey took the second mouse from Max. It looked like Apple except that it was a whole lot bigger. "Jenny might not believe me," Jeffrey said. "This mouse is so fat. But I guess it's worth a try."

Jeffrey started to run back to Mrs. Merrin's class with the new mouse. But a hand grabbed him.

"Now I know," Kenny said.

"Kenny!" Jeffrey was startled. "What are you doing here? And why did you lock me in the closet?"

"To set a trap, of course," Kenny said. "I wanted to see if the ghost would come and get you out of there. I waited around the corner and watched. Jeffrey, the doorknob turned *all by itself*! It was awesome. I *knew* it had to be a ghost!"

"Gee, Kenny. Didn't you feel the floor shake? There was an earthquake," Jeffrey said. "It jiggled the door open. I'll bet it measured eight on the Richter scale and probably one hundred on my bathroom scale."

Kenny thought about it for a minute. "Are you kidding, Jeffrey?" he asked.

Jeffrey didn't answer. He ran as fast as he could back to the classroom. "Jenny!" he shouted the minute he was inside. "Jenny, I've found Apple."

Jenny ran from her desk to meet Jeffrey. The whole class watched eagerly as she took the mouse in her hands. For a minute she was silent.

"Is it alive?" everyone asked.

"He's alive," Jenny said. "But, Jeffrey, why is he so fat?"

"I found him in the cafeteria, pigging out on sloppy joes," Jeffrey explained. "He's put on a few pounds." Jeffrey held his breath. Would she believe him?

Jenny smiled. "Thanks, Jeffrey," she said. "I'm really glad to have him back."

"Maybe you could change his name to Watermelon," Jeffrey said with a laugh as he walked to his seat.

A minute later, Kenny came back into the

room. "Jeffrey, you and I have got to talk—about you know what."

But before Jeffrey could answer, Mrs. Merrin sent Kenny to his seat. There were still sixteen more pets to show and tell about. It took the rest of the day.

Finally the school bell rang. It was time to go home.

"Jeffrey," Mrs. Merrin said from the front of the classroom. "Would you stay after school, please."

Another detention? Jeffrey thought. What did I do this time?

"Wait," Kenny complained to Jeffrey. "When are you going to tell me about the ghost?"

"Soon," Jeffrey said. "Soon."

The students and all of the animals slowly left the room. Only Jeffrey, Mrs. Merrin, and her puppy remained. Jeffrey and his teacher sat down next to the dog. It had fallen asleep on a pillow. As they sat down, Jeffrey saw Max appear. He was sitting on one of Mrs. Merrin's metal file cabinets. And he was petting his little mouse.

"That wasn't Apple, was it?" Mrs. Merrin asked.

Jeffrey was going to make up a story, but in-

stead he just shook his head. "Apple died," he said.

"Well, that was quick thinking," Mrs. Merrin said. "Also very generous, Jeffrey. Although I'll never know where you got that other mouse."

"Don't ask," said Jeffrey.

Mrs. Merrin nodded her head. "Well, anyway, that's not what I wanted to talk to you about," she went on. "I wanted to ask you a favor. My husband and I sometimes go away for weekends and we can't always take our puppy with us. So I thought maybe you could take care of him for us sometimes."

Jeffrey smiled. "That would be great."

"See what your parents say," Mrs. Merrin said.

"I don't have to ask them, Mrs. Merrin," Jeffrey said. "My parents always tell me to do *everything* my teacher says. And this time that will be coolsville with me!"

Here's a peek at Jeffrey's next adventure with Max, the third-grade ghost!

MAX ONSTAGE

"Now," said Mrs. Merrin, "would anyone like to volunteer to be the star alien in our class play?"

Almost before Mrs. Merrin finished her sentence, Kenny Thompsen's hand shot up in the air.

Jeffrey couldn't believe it—shy Kenny volunteering for the lead in a play—until he saw what happened. Max was standing beside Kenny, *raising* his hand *for* him! Of course, no one except Jeffrey could see the ghost. Max just looked at Jeffrey and laughed.

"Kenny, I'm surprised—pleasantly surprised," Mrs. Merrin said. "I'll be happy to give you the leading part. You'll be the star in our play about aliens from outer space."

Kenny's mouth flopped open and he couldn't say a word. He stared at his own arm, which was still being held up in the air. Finally he turned to Jeffrey. His face was pale and his voice was shaky. Something strange was going on, and he suddenly began to truly believe in Jeffrey's invisible friend, Max. "Jeffrey, help me. It's the ghost," Kenny whispered. "He won't let go of my arm!"

ABOUT THE AUTHORS

Bill and Megan Stine have written numerous books for young readers, including titles in these series: *The Cranberry Cousins; Wizards, Warriors, and You; The Three Investigators; Indiana Jones; G.I. Joe;* and *Jem.* They live on New York City's Upper West Side with their seven-year-old son, Cody, who believes in ghosts.